GROUP HUG

Written by
JEAN REIDY

Illustrated by
JOEY CHOU

GODWINBOOKS

Henry Holt and Company • New York

There once was a slug,
needing someone to hug.

SHRUG.

Along came a beetle,
a lonely ol' bug.

"You need a hug?
I have one," said Slug,
"to keep your heart snug!"

Nearby was Mouse
with a case of the grumps.

She'd hit a few bumps,
and was down in the dumps.

"Chin up," said Bug.
"There's no need to stew.
We'll help you pull through.
Your hug's overdue!"

GROUP HUG!

Then up shuffled Skunk,

lost control of his smell.

And Squirrel, as well,

had been sprayed. You could tell!

Their fragrance so foul,

proved hard to undo.

"Never mind the PEE-YOO,"

said Mouse. "Room for TWO!"

Now Beaver was busy,
too busy for friends.
When building his dam,
his job never ends.

"Take five! A quick break!"
said Squirrel and Skunk too.
"Come join our crew.
Let the hugging ensue!"

Along poked Porcupine,
feeling quite prickly.
I didn't say sickly,
just poky and prickly.

She needed a hug,
'cause hugs had been lacking.
Said Beaver, "Dear Porcupine—
send those quills packing!"

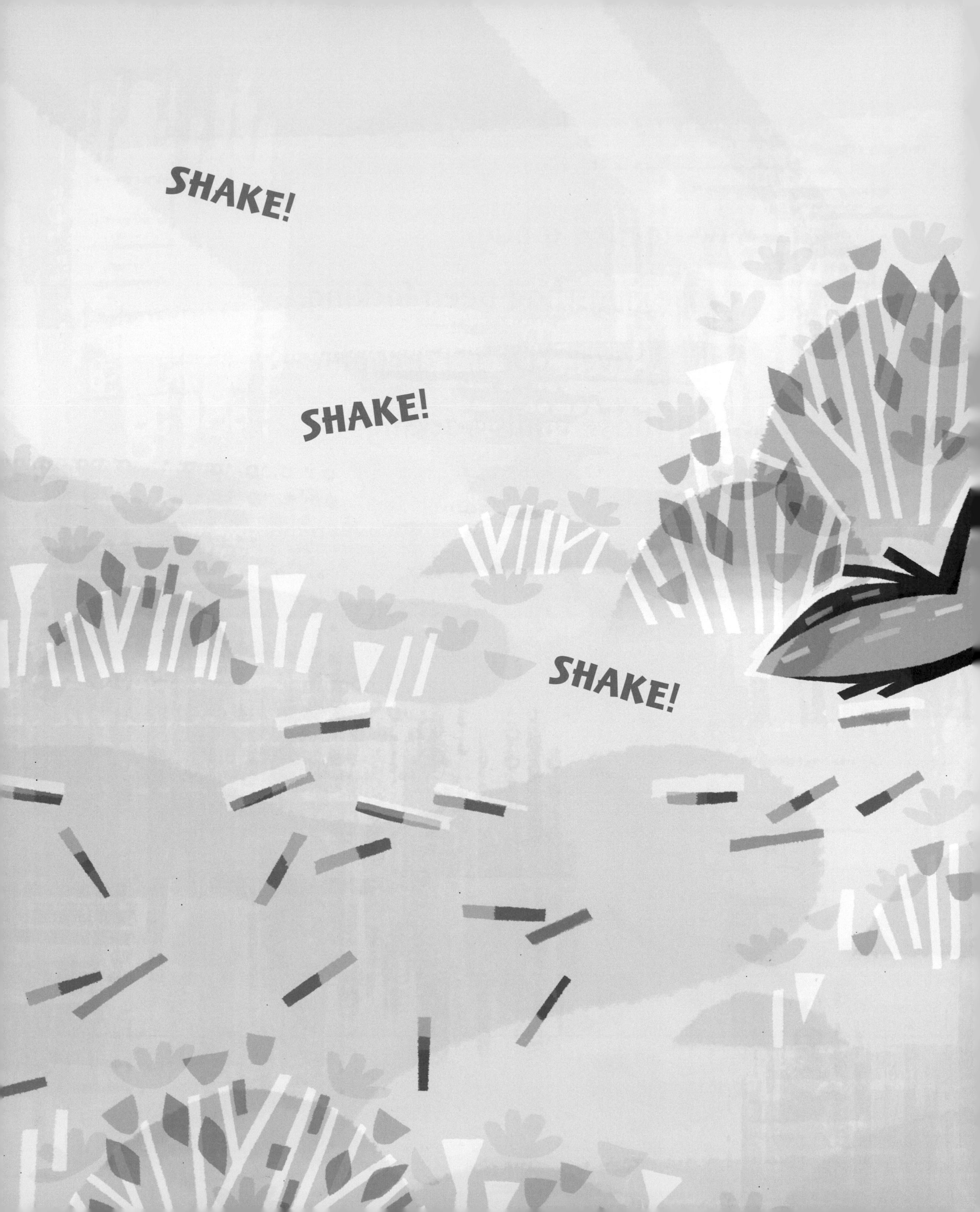

SHAKE!

SHAKE!

SHAKE!

GROUP HUG!

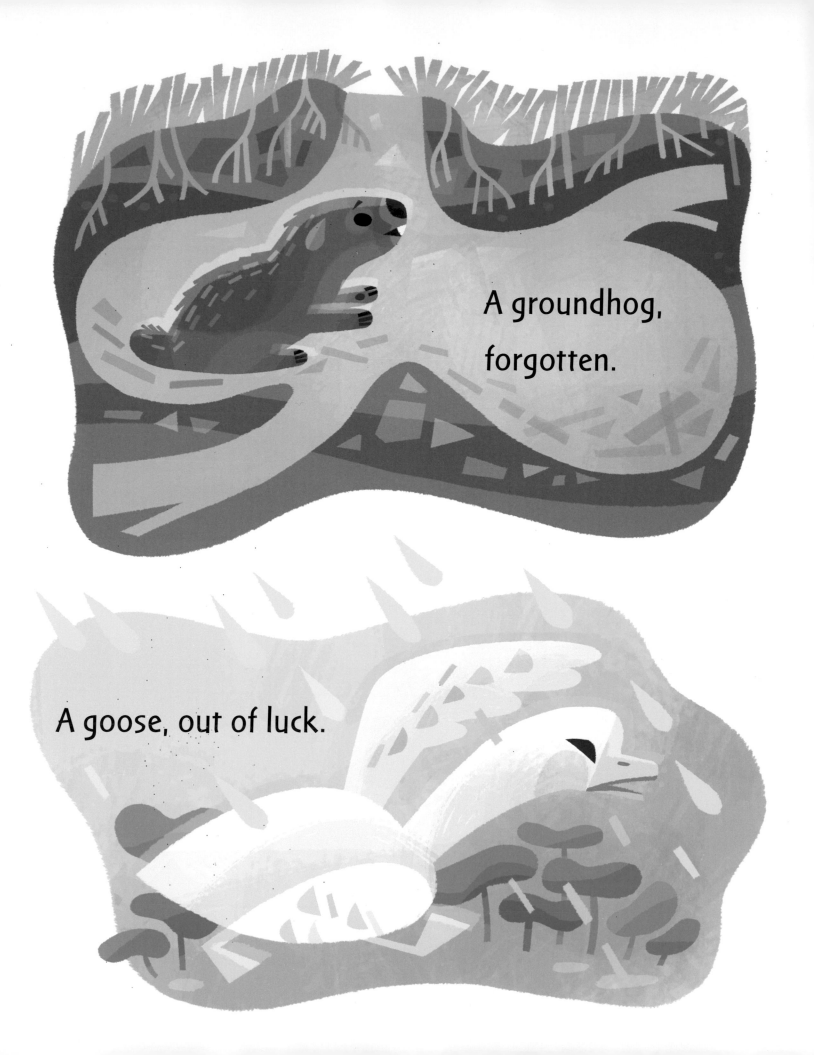

A groundhog,
forgotten.

A goose, out of luck.

A fox,

nicknamed "Sneaky."

A moose, feeling stuck.

The group hug stretched wide
and the group hug stretched tall,

making plenty of room
for those antlers and all.

Then . . .

along lumbered Bear
needing someone to care.
(Not to snack on, I swear.)
But they shouted . . .
"BEWARE!"

And off scampered Squirrel
and Skunk and the smell.

Off scooted Fox and Groundhog as well.

Off scurried Porcupine, no longer prickly.

Goose and Moose,

they skedaddled quite quickly.

Off skittered Mouse,

who was no longer blue.

And Beaver and Bug,

Bear scared them off too.

Till the only ones left
were that brave Slug and Bear.

And Slug said, "Hey there!
I've got hugs to spare."

See, that Slug knew a secret,
as sure as she'd shrugged . . .
that a hugger finds happiness . . .
'longside the hugged!

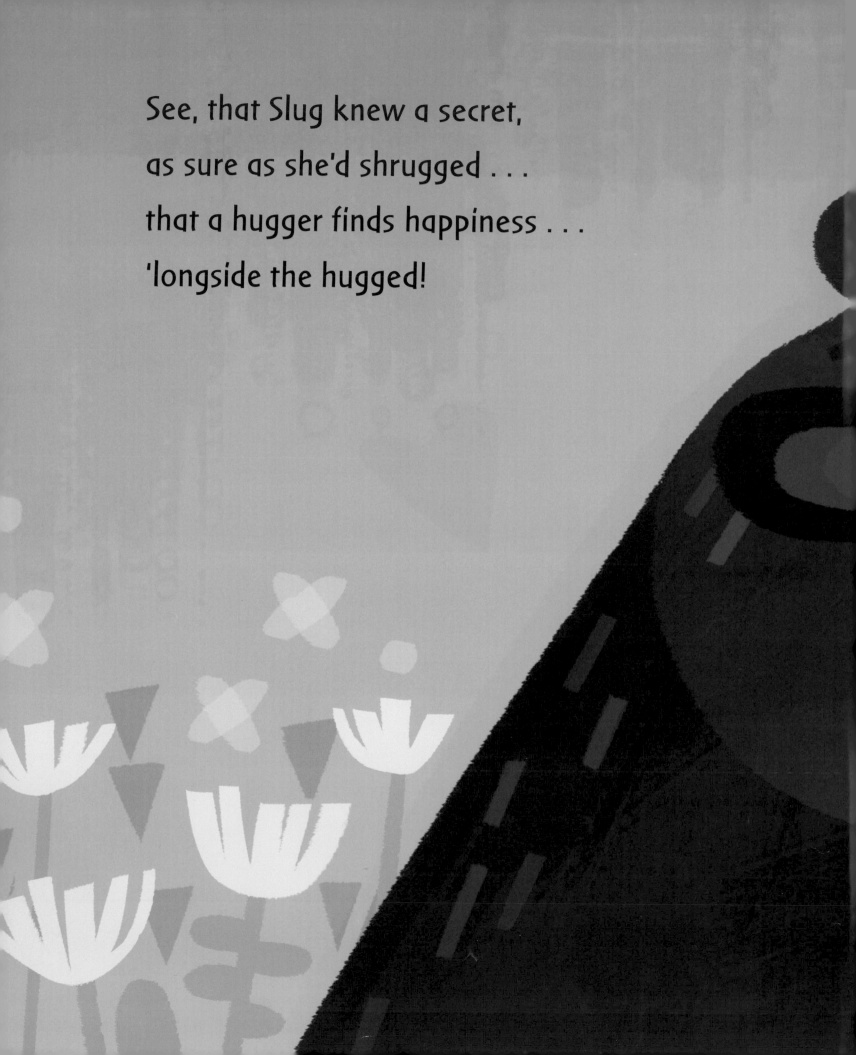

HEART TUG!

GROUP HUG!

To Charlie, with oodles of hugs! —J. R.

For Lemon and Kermit, thanks for all the hugs
when I needed them. —J. C.

Henry Holt and Company, *Publishers since 1866*
Henry Holt® is a registered trademark of Macmillan Publishing Group, LLC.
120 Broadway, New York, NY 10271
mackids.com
Text copyright © 2021 by Jean Reidy
Illustrations copyright © 2021 by Joey Chou
All rights reserved
Library of Congress Cataloging-in-Publication Data is available
Our books may be purchased in bulk for promotional, educational, or business use. Please contact your local bookseller
or the Macmillan Corporate and Premium Sales Department at (800) 221-7945 ext. 5442 or
by email at MacmillanSpecialMarkets@macmillan.com.
First Edition, 2021
Printed in China by RR Donnelley Asia Printing Solutions Ltd., Dongguan City, Guangdong Province

ISBN 978-1-250-12710-5
The art in this book was digitally painted using Photoshop.

1 3 5 7 9 10 8 6 4 2